Disney's

Winnie the Pooh

Make the Best of It

When things don't go

The way you plan,

Don't let that spoil your day.

Just make things work

The best you can–

You'll have more fun that way!

"Oh, my! I have so much to get ready!" said Piglet, scurrying about his little house. He had invited his friends over for haycorn muffins. It was going to be a very busy day!

“Oh, my, oh, dear,” worried Piglet. “What shall I do first?”

He began by sweeping his front yard. Then he was ready to make the haycorn muffins.

Piglet stood before his cupboard. It was looking rather empty. He was all out of flour and honey and haycorns!

"Oh, dear!" said Piglet. "I'll have to gather some haycorns. And borrow some honey and flour, too. I hope that won't take too long."

Piglet took his favorite basket outside, where a blustery wind was blowing haycorns onto the ground. Piglet had quickly filled his basket to the very top when Tigger suddenly bounced over to him.

"Hiya, Piglet Ol' Pal!" Tigger called.

Tigger's bounce completely emptied Piglet's basket!
"I was just gathering some haycorns," said Piglet sadly.
"Looks like you got plenty right here, Buddy Boy!" said Tigger.

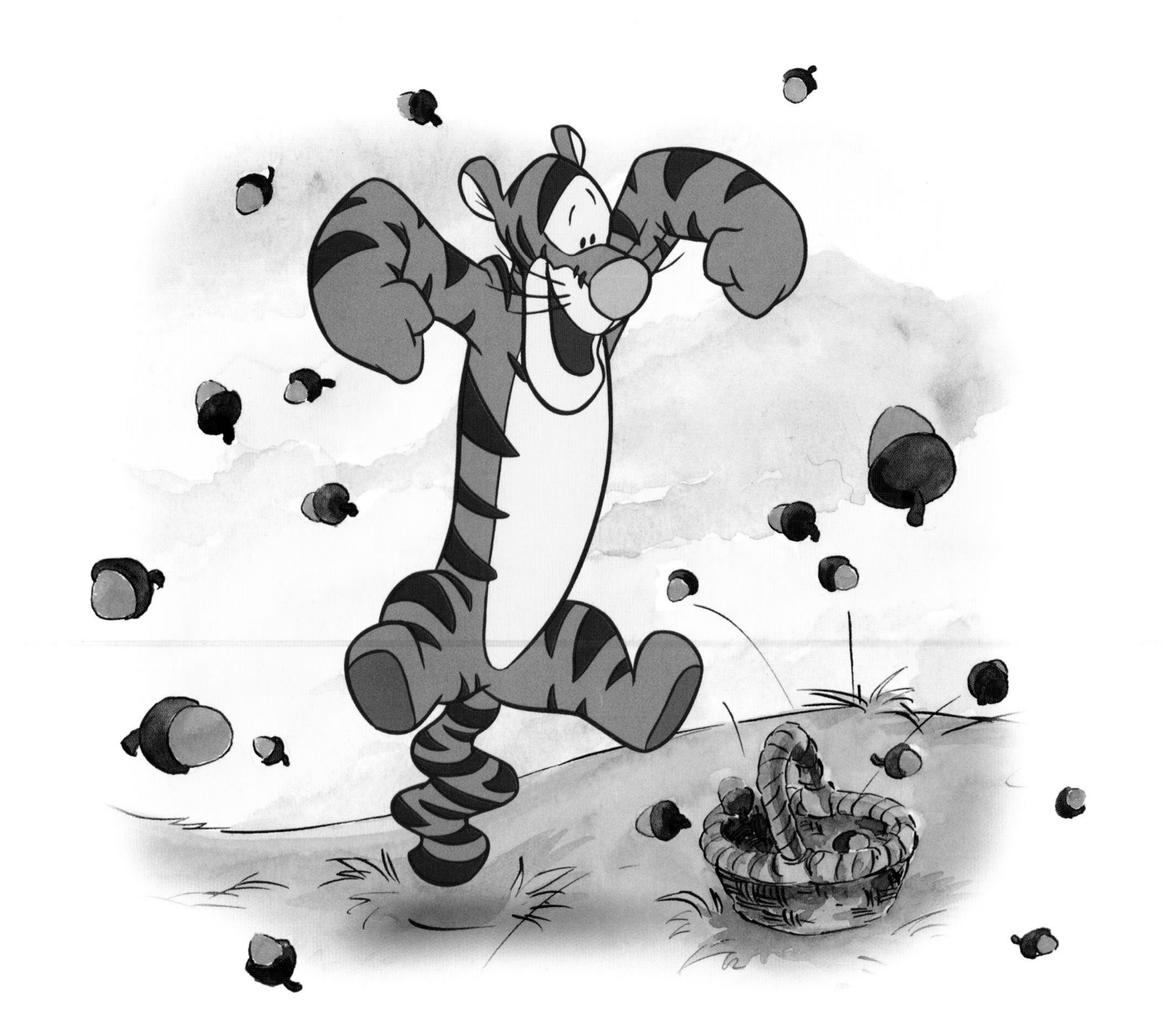

“Hey!” Tigger cried, gathering a bunch of haycorns. “Let me show you my basket-fillin’ bounce!” As Tigger bounced high into the air, he let go of the haycorns. They flew everywhere but into the basket.

"Well, gosh," said Tigger, "I wunner what's the matter with those silly haycorns? Let me give it another try."

"That's all right, Tigger," said Piglet. "I'll just fill the basket myself . . . again."

Piglet hadn't planned on gathering haycorns twice. And it took even longer to fill the basket this time.

"Oh, my," said Piglet, "it's getting rather late. I'll have to hurry if I want to borrow the flour and honey."

Piglet took the basket home and emptied all the haycorns. Then he ran over to Pooh's house.

"Pooh!" called Piglet. "May I borrow some honey?"

"Why, of course, Piglet," Pooh said in a muffled voice.

“But I’m afraid that this honey pot is rather empty,” sighed Pooh.

“It looks stuck. Let me help you, Pooh,” Piglet replied.

While Piglet pulled on the honey pot, Pooh pushed.

After a sticky struggle, the honey pot flew off with a big, loud POP! Pooh reached into his cupboard and handed Piglet a small honey pot.

"Oh, thank you, Pooh," said Piglet as he hurried off.

Next he went to Rabbit's to ask for some flour.

"Making your muffins?" Rabbit asked. "Do you mind if I come over and help?"

"That would be fine," Piglet agreed.

So the two friends headed back to Piglet's house.

While Piglet mixed the batter, Rabbit read the muffin recipe.

"Let's see," said Rabbit. "This recipe makes nine muffins. That means we can each have one."

“Unless, of course, you make a double batch,” Rabbit remarked. “Then we can each have two. Or a triple batch. Then we can each have three.” Rabbit was doing his muffin math.

As Piglet listened to Rabbit, he was so busy adding muffins in his head that he lost count of the baking powder. He put nine teaspoons in the batter instead of four! Poor Piglet didn't even realize what he had done.

After Rabbit left, Piglet put the muffins in the oven. The baking powder made the muffins rise . . . and rise . . . and rise!

When Piglet opened the oven, he saw one big gigantic muffin!

"Oh, dear!" said Piglet. "Nothing has gone the way I wanted it to today!"

Piglet felt awful. His muffin party was ruined!

Piglet stared hopelessly at his muffin-cake. Maybe he could break it into muffin pieces. No, he decided, they would look too strange. Maybe he could just send everyone home. No, he thought, that wouldn't be very polite.

“Oh, dear,” Piglet said to himself. “What would Pooh do?” There must be some way to save the muffin-cake.

“I’ve got it!” Piglet cried, clapping his hands.

Piglet went back to work. He took out several bowls to make frosting in pink, purple, orange, red, green, and blue. Piglet took his time and frosted the cake very carefully.

When Piglet was done, he stood back to look at his cake. "Oh, my! It's not so bad after all!" he said. Then, with a smile on his face, he finished cleaning up. Minutes later, all his friends appeared at his door.

"Those muffins smell absoposolutely wonderful, Little Buddy!" cried Tigger. "Let me at 'em!"

"Well, actually," Piglet replied, "we're not having muffins."

"Not having muffins?" gasped Rabbit. "Whatever do you mean?"

Piglet led his friends over to the table. Nobody said a word—that is, until they saw Piglet's amazing muffin-*cake*.

"Why, Piglet!" said Kanga. "What a beautiful cake!"

"I'll say! Simply splendiferous, Piglet Ol' Pal!" Tigger cried.

Piglet had decorated a part of the cake for each of his friends.

"The muffins didn't turn out the way I planned," Piglet explained. "So I tried to make the best of things."

Pooh smiled at his friend. “You certainly did, Piglet,” he agreed.

And as the friends shared the muffin-cake, even Piglet had to admit—it was the best haycorn treat he had ever made.

A LESSON A DAY POOH'S WAY

When things don't go

the way you plan,

make the best of it.